FRAGMENTS
of Leukippus

Atoms (1993 collage on photopaper)

FRAGMENTS
of Leukippus

A. M. Caratheodory

Tyborne Hill &
Calliope Press
2007

Acknowledgments
Cambridge University Press, for selections on Leukippus from
        The Pre-Socratic Philosophers, by G. S. Kirk and J. E. Raven, 1957.
Harvard University Press, for selections on Demokritus from Ancilla to
        the Pre-Socratic Philosophers by Kathleen Freeman, 1947.

The Argonaut, for "First Phoenix" (1975)
Best Poets/20th Century, "Shadow of the Mistress of the World" (1977)
Sawtooth, for "Amaryllis" (1977)
Transition for "Dionysius's Dream" (1977)
Snapdragon for "Children of Ankaa" (1977)
Palouse for "Tantalus" and "Anteus and Herakles" (1980)
Windrow for "Aekus Humbled" and "Stair of Iris" (1983)
Amphibian Dreams for "The Others" and "Heraklitus's Dream" (1983)

Publisher's Cataloging-in-Publication data
Alain Menarde Caratheodory, 1946—
Fragments of Leukippus / A. M. Caratheodory
I. Title.
PS3553.F644F766 2007
ISBN 0-911385-09-6 (paper)
Manufactured in the United States of America

Second Printing

A Calliope Press Book
Mozart and Reason Wolfe, Ltd., Wilmington, Delaware
www.3musesbooks.com

Ebook version
Tyborne Hill, Palo Alto, California
www.tybornehill.com

FRAGMENTS

Dedication

Ad Johanna Metzger

Me iuvet hesternis positum languere corollis,
quem tetigit iactu certus ad ossa deus.

Propertius

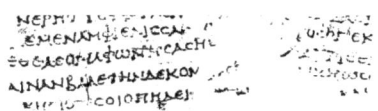

Introduction

F ire, water, air, and even earth have treated the writings of the ancient Greeks very poorly. Texts have disappeared by accident, through neglect, and by intention. There is little hope of finding original papyrus manuscripts in mainland Greece; they cannot survive even that relatively dry climate. Only in the waterless parts of Egypt, buried in rubbish heaps, tombs, or cities beneath the sands, can finds be expected.

In 1961, however, an original papyrus was discovered in continental Greece at Dervani (Lagada). The story of that rare find is recorded by Herbert Hunger, "Papyrusfund in Griechenland," *Chronique D'Egyopte*, tome XXXVII, number 74, July 1962. Then, in July 1973, another manuscript, completely unrelated, was found in earthenware within 300 meters of the same site. This second manuscript was badly deteriorated; no single scrap was preserved complete, and few pages kept their integrity. The manuscript was identified as a missing work of Leukippus. It is translated and presented for the first time.

Of all the works of the pre-Socratics assembled by translators from Diels to Kirk and Raven, the major name missing has always been Leukippus, the founder of atomistic philosophy. Commentators of the ancient world have reported the activities of Leukippus—Simplicius (Phys. 28,4; R546), Hyppolytus (Ref. 1,13,2; R 564), Aetius (IV,8; R 586), and Cicero (Academica pr. 11,37,118; R 548)—but there were too few sources of material. Hyppolytus reports that Leukippus was a hearer of Zeno the Eliatic, but did not follow his doctrine (1 12). Simplicius states that Leukippus attended the courses of the Eliatics, but did not accept their teachings and went in the opposite direction (*Phys.* 28,4). More than one philosopher and commentator has dismissed his existence as mythical. Diogenes Laertius, for example, states, "He and Hemarchus both maintain that there never was a philosopher Leukippus, who, some ... say, was the teacher of Democritus" (X,13; R 547, Raven's translation).

Leukippus is a shadowy figure in early Greek philosophy. *His fame, like the rays of an older, faded star in a double star system, has been eclipsed and absorbed by the clearer and brighter light of his pupil, Demokritus, through which faint lines have been transmitted to us.* It is believed that Leukippus was born before 493 B.C., or forty years after Anaxagoras, who was born in 533 B.C., and that Leukippus was, in turn, forty years older than Demokritus. Other commentators have put Leukippus as a close contemporary of Demokritus and estimated that he was in his prime about 430 B.C. It is believed that Leukippus came to Abdera from Miletus, but two other cities are sometimes listed as his place of birth. The facts of his existence may never be known for certain.

Speculations about the Origin of the Theory
There is a curious tradition (Strabozvi, p. 757) that the atomic theory originat-
ed with "Mochus," a Phoenician philosopher said to have lived about the time
of the Trojan War, and that he founded a school that lasted at least until the
Fourth Century A.D. This tradition is usually rejected as a fable.

At an early date, Indian philosophers arrived at an atomic explanation
of the universe. The doctrines of this school were expounded in the *Vaicesika
Sutra* and interpreted by the aphorisms of Kanada. Like the pre-Socratics, they
reached such a position through the denial of the possibility of infinite division
and the assertion that indivisible particles must be reached to secure reality
and permanence in the world. There are considerable differences between the
doctrines, however. The Indian atoms are not all homogenous, but correspond
to the elements that they compose (earth, air, fire, water) and their qualities
vary accordingly. The atoms are conceived as being elastic in structure. Kanada
works out their combinations in a detailed system reminiscent of Pythagoras.
It is improbable that there was any cross-pollination of ideas. One authority
maintains that there is no proof of the atomic doctrine in India until after contact with the Greek kingdom of Bactria. The dates have not been fixed.

Unlike their contemporaries in India and China, the pre-Socratics did
not think exegetically, placing their ideas in a scriptural context. Instead, they
spoke as thinking individuals, often disrespectful of poets, priests, and other
thinkers, claiming only the authority of reason. Dissatisfaction with the traditional answers to perpetual questions may have been the start of philosophy.
The appeal to reason allowed Leukippus to subject the thought of his predecessors to criticism and revision, to alter it and to go beyond it. His successors,
of course, claimed the same privilege.

Previously, it was difficult to separate the theories of Leukippus from
those of Demokritus. If these fragments are proved authentic, then the theory
underwent considerable modification by Demokritus and others, as will become evident.

The Synthesis
Leukippus was the inheritor and critic of all the theories that came before him.
Anaximander first postulated an indeterminate material that could not be perceived as the arche, the ultimate underlying substance. Heraklitus noted that all
things flowed. Pythagoras proved the plural mathematical basis of nature. Then,
Parmenides fused the changing experiences of the sensory world into one
undifferentiated, timeless, changeless being. This radical repudiation of tradition
and common sense described reality as a perfect sphere excluding change and
nonbeing. Many subsequent philosophers devoted themselves to showing how
change was possible at all.

Empedokles synthesized the thoughts of his predecessors into a theory of mixture and separation. The water of Thales, the air of Anaximenes, the
fire of Heraklitus, and earth were mixed and separated by strife and love in the
great ages of the world. Anaxagoras taught that everything consisted of an infinite number of seeds, and that, although there was a portion of everything in all

things, the majority of seeds making up a thing determined what it was—rock, finger, or tree. The motion and direction of things were determined by mind. This plurality of the types of basic substance by Empedokles and Anaxagoras violated the Eleatic dictum that true being was one.

The dilemma of Leukippus was how to solve the difficulties of the Milesians, to incorporate the values of the pluralists, and still satisfy the propositions of the Eleatic school, that is, how to solve the problems of being and not-being, becoming and dissolution, change and motion, and sense perception and ideas. The influence of Zeno and the younger Eleatics is clear. There is a tradition preserved by Tzetzes that Leukippus was a pupil of Melissus, whose criticisms foreshadowed the atomic theory.

Like Empedokles and Anaxagoras, Leukippus shattered the Eleatic sphere into pieces, but he did not color the fragments with dyes from the sensible world, with the fire and water and rainbow perceptions of sensible reality. The pieces lay in the Eleatic simplicity, like bits of a perfect glass globe, producing the flat, dense black of a frozen lake on a starless night. *And what the stiff logic of Parmenides refused, what the dynamic imagination of Empedokles did not conceive—what Aristotle never allowed—Leukippus did. He made a gap in nature.* He made a nonbeing in which the identical atoms could move, and temporarily stalled the wheels of controversy.

It seems so simple. The Eleatic criticism of the theories of the Pythagoreans led Leukippus logically to the atomic solution. The whole physical setting of the theory and its view of the physical substratum of existence was inherited from the Ionian monists and the pluralists. Leukippus established a unity that allowed an infinite multiplicity, yet provided an underlying unity.

The Theory

All reality is reduced to atoms. The atoms are completely full and perfectly hard; they are uncuttable. The atoms are the same in substance and identical; they are mathematically divisible, but not physically divisible. They are unities—an infinite number of identical, full spheres. (Unaccountably, the words '*ne atomos*' are feminine.)

Then, no less real than the fullness, entangled throughout the atoms and where they were not, is the infinite void. A nothingness stretched out by fullness, and as necessary, backing the fullness, allowing change and motion. The nothingness is just as primary; it also is indivisible and unchanging. The nothingness is necessary to explain movement, to explain the contraction and expansion of solids. The nothingness woven with atoms explains why an experimenter could pour the same amount of water into a vessel of ashes as into an empty vessel of the same size. Animals and vegetables can grow without losing their shape only by intussuseption; the interstices expand for food; otherwise only the surface would grow and we would all become spheres with thickened skin. As Burnet points out, the concept of noncorporeal existence is a strange achievement for the founder of the great materialist school of antiquity.

Leukippus assumed that the atoms were in intrinsic motion through the nothingness. The motion is eternal and natural. One cannot ask the reason for it any more than one can ask the reason for atoms and nothingness. Wisely, Leukippus did not offer any reasons. As Burnet supplies, it is when motion had to be introduced as the cause of the separation of an originally compact mass, whose nature was motionless and continuous, that it was necessary to explain its origin.

An infinite number of atoms moves eternally through a space infinite in extent. By their unregulated impetus they collide, and by mutual plaiting bring about worlds and their contents. An infinite number of worlds may be created. All things are created by the entanglement of the atoms and their oscillation. Atoms in contact form bodies. Even when the atoms are in contact with one another in a compound body their motions continue. They perform tiny trajects, according to the nature of the compound, colliding and recoiling again to another collision. Everything that we perceive through the senses is in a constant state of internal vibration.

Atoms can differ in position and arrangement to one another. Leukippus gives us "rhythm," "touching," and "turning" as technical terms to explain atomic relationships. If one factor only is altered, a different substance is obtained, as tragedy and comedy use the same letters in the alphabet. Other differences may be derived from the amount of nothingness between atoms.

Leukippus states that the atoms have contact, but do not merge. Anaxagoras anticipated complete fusion in his idea of "mixture," but Leukippus believed that fusion would destroy the basis of permanence. Mixing is sufficient to account for all the variety of phenomena, as well as for infinite complexity.

The Pythagoreans suggested the indefiniteness of matter, in contradistinction with form. Plato contrasted the impermanent stuff of the world with rigid, unchangeable ideas. Leukippus offers us unchangeable atoms and indefinite and impermanent compounds. This is not antithetical. Leukippus has reduced the forms to one: The sphere. He even uses the word eidos or "form" interchangeably with atom. As can be said, "everywhere it flows." The world we swim in is a qualitative expression of a serene, immutable quantity.

Leukippus envelopes the world in a membrane or caul formed by the entangling of atoms in a vortex. He may have borrowed the idea of a whirl from Anaxagoras, where it was the rotary motion communicated by mind to portions of the mixture. This metaphor, which resembles the nebular hypothesis of Kant, is used to explain both large and small-scale phenomena. The vortex sounds like a combination of gravitational and electrical spin. Although Leukippus mentions levels of order and grades of existence, he does not elaborate on them, and they remain unsophisticated concepts.

On the other hand, his cosmology is interesting and sophisticated. Pythagoras and Anaximander, for example, regarded the world as a kosmose, that is, an ordered, visible "all." Empedokles and Plato called the world a holon, after the Stoics, for whom a holon was a kosmos ruled by logos. Leukippus named the whole a systema, whose parts combined to produce more than the mere sum of parts, as color arises from colorless atoms. The earth, sun, and planets were one systema; the stars were real items in other universes. The term universe, by the way, arose from Cicero's reading of holon. Interestingly,

Arthur Koestler has made a scientific term of holon, which also has a place in Ludwig von Bertalanffy's general systems theory. Having pointed out some of the parallels with Leukippus' terminology, we will not elaborate them here.

The universe of Leukippus is the order and chaos of atoms entering and leaving aggregations. Order is violated by disorder according to the laws of combination and dissolution. A harmony arises from the blending of opposites: Being and nonbeing, order and chaos.

Leukippus seemed to take the old Ionian ideas of cosmology uncritically at first, but then changed his mind and derived the best of the ideas from the Eleatics concerning the shape of the earth and the importance of the sun and moon. As Plutarch said of Demokritus and Aristotle, Leukippus was willing to renounce without fuss or irritation views formerly held and found to be mistaken.

Leukippus' theory of vision is a sophisticated version of Empedokles'. Eidola ("What one sees" from Homer) flow off things; these shaped images enter the eye. In fact, all perception is dependent on contact. The senses used properly are safe guides to truth. Indeed, the truth lay in appearances. The body is altered by contact with its surroundings; the surroundings are different with the body in them. Unlike the logos, which was of a rational nature and appeared behind the phenomena, the nature of Leukippus was something that one added to. The history of an atom could change its rhythm; aggregations and compound bodies had histories. The mind creates patterns in nature because it is a pattern of collisions of atoms. The soul creates ethics because it is a part of the flow of nature. In Leukippus' words, it: "achieves unity as it passes through the body."

The attitude of Leukippus towards the soul is unique. It is the most deli-cate of atomic combinations and the most likely to fall apart. Doubtless crude social actions could destroy it. Unfortunately, most of his Ethics and Politics is lost. His views on theory, in which the senses perceive themselves to create a new level of ideas, is also unique and does not seem to have survived Demokri-tus' interpretations. The skepticism concerning religion and the gods is quite typical of the times.

The series of genuine fragments toward the end of the book are separate poems possibly written for local contests. "The Others" may have been written by a student, or perhaps Leukippus' old age overlapped Plato's youth. The dates are uncertain. The parentage is uncertain, but the poem offers a Dionysian contrast to Plato's *Republic*.

The Place of the Theory
For the pre-Socratics, humanness was still a part of nature, not standing in contradiction to or superior to the nonhuman world, but as a component of it. Humanity lived by the ordinances that ruled all things; ethics was implicit. Law was nourished by natural law. Aristotle characterized all this as the "philosophy of nature" and said that *mythos* and *logos*, myth and reason, overlapped in the philosophies of these shadowy (to him) precursors. He noted that they were poets as often as philosophers.

It was thought that poets erred by encouraging men to accept transitory experience as having ultimate validity. Yet, today a philosophical poet may be more appropriate than Aristotle. *The poet lives in language, the image of the world, but the philosopher lives constantly in the shadow of infidelity, suspecting metaphor or tautology, or succumbing to the ultimate despair, fear that she is dealing with arbitrary names. The poet describes, but the philosopher has to conclude. Poets trust names and can be playful and assured; philosophers need to be right.* Though language is changing, descriptions prove to be more true than conclusions.

Leukippus' poetic nature can be compared to Goethe's. Goethe's concepts did not deny individuality: Nature is like an infinite space, which though itself formless, produces individual forms everywhere. *Eidos* in Goethe was thought to be true being; the eidos is the heart and the heart eidos. Nature is still an open secret that the discerning eye can learn. Goethe and Leukippus are far removed from the modern conception of the physical sciences. They sought ideas capable of comprehending the world and the mind, of understanding the whole, as well as each individual. And, their ideas were based on metaphorical thinking.

Modern Parallels of the Theory
Leukippus made one of the fundamental presuppositions of modern science: Qualitative difference and change can be expressed in purely quantitative and geometrical terms. His metaphor of atoms is the basis for modern atomic theory. It is tempting to build unimagined bridges between widely separated thoughts. It is also tempting to read into the fragments a great anticipation of modern science, which is not there. Nevertheless, a brief examination of the parallels of thought is in order.

Leukippus' world is made up of a collection of wholes; each whole is an atom. There was no experimental support for his hypothesis. In Dalton's 1808 hypothesis, the atoms of a chemical element were all identical; they combined in different proportions to make up molecules of different sorts. His hypothesis was confirmed by experiments. The complex characteristics of chemical elements were explained in terms of a few building blocks—not entirely unlike the blocks of Leukippus. Then, the atom was discovered to have constituents: An electron and a nucleus. The Bohr atom was a paradox. It was indivisible by nature, but had moveable parts, which were discovered by Rutherford. Bohr paraphrased Aristotle when he said that "it is a great mistake to speak more precisely than your knowledge." It was Bohr who proposed the principle of complementarity, the use of two mutually exclusive approaches to fully describe a situation (light, for instance, both a wave and a particle). The dichotomies of Leukippus also remained distinct, change and permanence, being and nonbeing. The atom was still "uncuttable" with parts. Atoms were still discrete particles associated to constitute a given material.

Atomic theory still guides the development of modern scientific hypotheses. It persists in doctrines as revolutionary as Albert Einstein's and John Wheeler's. Its features may be detected behind the novel disguise of point-events separated in 'space-time' by 'interval-relations' following a 'geodesics'. But, physics has abandoned the atom for other more elementary particles. There are over 500 elementary particles as subatomic constituents of matter. How many particles are possible is still yet unknown.

Sometimes the only difference between modern particles are charge or spin. Particles are what they do, which is move. They are not the immutable points of matter ascribed to Leukippus. Every level of particle seems to be made of something more basic. Quarks are constituents of hadrons. Baryons are variants of the proton. All particles may be equally fundamental and elementary. Furthermore, at ultra-high temperatures, all particles may be the same; at absolute zero, however, atoms may be basic. Ultimately, some theory may reduce the differences to a one-dimensional constant, the Planck mass, for instance. The vagueness of Leukippus' atom allows it to be interpreted at any level, from quark to atom. Does the name of the ultimate unit matter, if there is one unit? Is thinking about nature more important than looking at it?

Some of Leukippus' ideas have appeared in modern times in a variety of disciplines. His turning (trope) is a precursory notion of allotropic modification, or isomery, in inorganic chemistry. The same turning on a metaphysical level anticipates an idea in Twentieth-century French phenomenology   (Merleau-Ponty). His ethics book, *Tritogenia*, on the three-fold origin of things, seems similar to the "Threeness" of the pragmaticist, Charles Sanders Peirce.

Science is in need of a Leukippus, to resolve dilemmas by imaginative leaps, to extend a vision of reality through an imaginative model of the universe, to live deeply in metaphor, exploring philosophical possibilities. Other commentators warn their readers not to see not to see modern implications in ancient speculative theories—perhaps rightly so—but there is a greater danger that, in the midst of calculation, regard for the imagination and the importance of history may suffer, and a dull, philosophical amnesia may turn our efforts in circles. The ideas of Leukippus are still meaningful today, even if the terminology and the science do not fit perfectly. Although modern physics has spawned limitless particles from the atom and given atomism a reductionistic nature, the principle is unchanged—there are basic particles that combine to flower into the manifold profusion of the universe; particles are whole forms; humans are complex forms with rules for living together.

The Translation
The most formidable problem in translating from Greek has been to find a just approximation of Greek stanza forms and meter. There can never be a single correct solution for the transfer of prosodic techniques from one language to another. This is one interpretation by a mind sympathetic in spirit and steeped in the attitude of the times.

Much Greek philosophy and poetry was composed to be heard, sung, chanted, or recited, and not read. In the original papyrus scripts the words were all run together as in Sanskrit. The poetic lines were also run together, and only capital letters were used. Therefore, the question of whether English lines should be capitalized has no real precedence in the original scripts. A sample line from the manuscript, in strict translation, would look like this:

'WHEREISARCHITECTOFCAVES'.

I have tried to giver order to these translations in several ways. To approximate the easy, conversational flow of many of the phrases, I often have given a syllabic rather than an accentual regularity to the lines. The Greeks wrote—and spoke—in a language that was natural and contemporary to their readers and listeners. My intention has been to use a classical, formal English to do justice to the magnitude of the ideas, and a chaste, contemporary idiom when necessary.

The Greeks did not use end rhyme as a common poetic device, although it was used rarely for humor or satire, so rhyme is not used in these translations. I have tried to retain the stanzas or paragraphs suggested by the metrical stops in the texts. I have also tried to present the equivalent of Greek, literally. In most cases the Greek and not the Latin form of spelling has been used. In most cases I have supplied titles for informational purposes based on the context. This is a traditional translator's prerogative. A few titles— 'Cosmology,' 'Tritogenia'—are standard in Greek philosophy. The numbered sections in the Ethics are Freeman's translations of Demokritus's interpretative texts based on Leukippus; the originals are identical. Few ancient authors cited sources or marked quotations.

Leukippus exhibits a genius for the invention of striking and quaint technical terms, in contrast to the more universal and detailed diligence of his student, Demokritus. I have tried to be faithful to these terms. Cicero said that Demokritus's style had rhythm; the style of Leukippus has no less of a unique rhythm. I have used the word "particles" to replace the original "atoms" to avoid present-day connotations and possible confusion with the new atomic theory.

The selections presented here are not complete. Thirty one unrelated or irrelevant fragments have been omitted. For example,

14.3 "Arkturus—rainbearer."

These may be reviewed at a later date.

I have discovered, in my digging, *fragments like pieces of a statue*—a bare torso, exquisitely wrought, from which the head, hands, arms, and legs have been torn by time. I have unearthed the fragments and gathered them together, curious about the face's expression and how the limbs were arranged. The part is a monument to the whole thought, conveying the absence, but bringing an exhilarating presence—not really needing more. The poverty of a lacuna-ridden text contributes a poignancy and quality of modernity that a completely reconstructed text would lack. Incomplete passages, whose original context is lost, lend a mysterious quality to the fragments and invite the imagination to fit possibilities to them. The fragments present half of a dialogue that we are free to enter. We now face the same questions raised in the texts: Being, time, growth, decay, love, language, family, society, and thought.

Complete Poems

46. *The Others*

"When he recalled his first home and the wisdom there,
And his fellow prisoners in that time, don't you suppose
He would consider himself happy for the change and pity
The others?"

Platon, Republic VII 516e

The world is washed with light; sky and rock
Are bleached white. There is the sea
And the faded green of trees.

To be as you taught, we thought we advanced
Toward perfection, but we became weary and lost—
Our tongues dried out. We perceived nothing
But intervals of light. We could not reach
Your ideal.... [nor] erase our origins.
You called us strange prisoners bound by our legs
And necks before shadows cast on the side
Of the cave by fires. You thought you freed
Us and dragged us up a rough, steep path.
You forced us to see the sun, source of the seasons
And steward of all things in the visible world.
From there we were led to contemplation of
What is best in the things that truly are.

But when we recalled our first home,
We longed for a world without weather,
Away from relentless, sun-driven change.
We longed to escape the weight of truth—
And then we found the cave again.
Let the hills take that unbearable mass
From our shoulders. Let the damp restore
Moisture to our skins and the dark
Return our dreams.

The abyss opened under our feet;
All we wanted from you, Platon, had not
The power to raise us higher—the dialectic
Does not lead upward, or outward;
There is no up or down, in or out,
Only the continuing spiral onward.

Where is the architect of the cave,
Whom we once praised? Welcome us back
With new designs. Make walls to keep
The sun from our eyes. We will use shadows
And mirrors to freeze its awful visage.

This is the place of life—the caves
Are not vacant, as the plains above.
We have made the earth secure with our
Own dark geography, comfortably bound.
This is our fathers' hearth. Savor
The aroma of cooking lamb—the senses
Expand—hear the trickle of water seeking
Its level through chiaroscuro rooms.

The caves are home. In filtered light
We polish the walls lustrous ...
Ordained in the wombs of our mothers
To sow doubt in the entrails of the earth.
We meditate in the depths and sleep
In the [narcotic] knowledge of rock. Mysteries
Leak into dreams inverted in negative infinity.

We press the limits of darkness down
To the limits of our illusions, insert
Ourselves in crevices of being—[matter's]
Center and the heart's, invisible.
We burrow in the [solidity] of rock
And build temples to feeling.

You taught us that the activity of art
Had the power to release us,
But art has its roots in darkness
And though its surface is displayed
For all, it seeks to intertwine things
With invisibility that we may see them.
We must play with shadows and live between
Perfect light and darkness, a double life.
This is the true song of the dialectic
Weaving voices into silence and twining
All things opposite around an empty center.

The sun impales forms; their colors
Are burned off. Light decomposes flesh
And only proud skeletons remain.

Wisdom is a wild thing like the Arcadian doe
And not easily captured with words. The dappled
Form leaves its shadow in our grasp while it slips
Away undaunted. A hunger we do not understand
Keeps us on the scent. We cannot give up the chase—
Nor can we ever catch her. [So] to be wise,
We must act as if the shadow is the doe.

Hephaestus
Agonistes

Dusty hero approached dusty hero
along a dusty road—at
first equally matched
sinews popped and sweat ran

But Antaeus drew his strength
from his mother the earth and slowly
[prevailed] against his opponent with
a laugh. Herakles was bent backwards
until, almost broken, he thought—

He swung and lifted Antaeus off the ground
and choked him as his strength grew feeble
the strong limbs wilting in air.
water conquers earth.

You are our nemesis, Herakles,
for you are strong enough and cunning
to separate us from the source
of our strength, the earth.

But we are Herakles as well and strangle
ourselves, punished by the gods
for our pride in individual power.
... [now] fire waits.

32. *Tantalus*

The [citrus] rolls and falls off
the table and rolls under it—
the thought retreats

We reach for particles and stars
and they recede
beyond our grasp.

Everything is made of particles
full of strangeness and [charm]
that we cannot possess.

Trees lift fruit beyond our reach
and water recedes from our thirst—
it is our desires that offend

33. *Heraklitus's Dream*

The earth turns; sun lights forests
and fields, and they breathe;
[matter] feels.

Pines transform light to [honey].
Then the earth turns from the sun
and the forest exhales.

Leaves disappear in flames
invisibly, radiating heat at night.
The forest is a burning house—
whole mountains burn coldly,
more slowly than stars.

Life is fire, and it does
not need a body of its own;
it dies and is reborn in everything.

We live by the interior touch of flame,
tenuous flame, dissolving weight;
fire is the [thing] in bloom.

34. *Phoenix*

You were born on the wind from burning day
Your wings and feathers from shafts of light
Your beak obsidian, your talons shards of ice
You only—there could be no other.
You flew [aloft] for hundreds of years
Alone, not wanting [not] needing rest.
You searched the desert for hundreds more
For the palm to build your nest.
From aromatic limbs you wove a pyre
And waited for the fire to rise.
You preened your crimson plumage
And rested your ancient eyes.
You shrilled an alien song:
The sun's rays focused—ignited a root.
You fanned your wings and uttered cries
As the palm tree burned with its red fruit.

Calm companion of heat, you know the complexion
Of flames. You rose from genetic ashes
Feathers fired, a spectrum from the white.
You will live as long as the sun
Setting and rising from the palm
The same yet new until there is nothing
Left but the palm in blackened skies,
Then the ashes will cool, the song will end.

35. *The Shadow of the Mistress of the World*

It is the way—all movement turns to heat;.
You burn and rise from the ashes.

As the phoenix burns the wind stirs
The ashes and rises—
The sky darkens with torrential rain
But the [helix] turns, the code remains.

The ashes expand and steam; something
Moves and fights its way out—
Dark nebula—
Molten red metallic bird renewed.

Particles burn, particles fuse
Fire phoenix, you grow
Wood, earth, metal phoenix.

You grow and your shadow grows
Still larger. Order and [heat]
Create complexity in ashes.

Your feathers are now metallic
You alter yourself to survive
But only you notice the change
And the change is irreversible.

How much of your life does
The shadow take as its own?

We dream of darkness
And build buildings without windows.
We fear fire
And bury our dead in bronze and stone
Remembering what Heraklitus
Saw in the hearth—
The spirit of the forge, defender
Against beasts and cold
And dark, but, too, our possible
Annihilation beyond bones.

Our oldest myths are myths of the sun.
We have memories of perfect forms
And abstract them still
From cloudy images.
We long to see ghosts in metal
And powers of healing in trees.

We are fascinated by the myriad faces
Of [energy] and court their embraces
In our searching.
The earth is our body and our body
A burning house—our blood is red
With heat, our skin the color of ashes.
We are the ashes of stars;
When we are dead
Who knows what will rise.

37. *Birth of Mercury*

... the moon rose over black hills and felt
along the ridge with its light until it found
the river ... phoenix rose ... twining a ray
and covering the moon with her wings ...
to a distant mountain ... lay waiting

The sun pushed day over [blue-grey] hills
and followed the river to the plain ... to
mounds of shallow sulfur and burned the lion
free ... [who] traveled relentlessly toward ...

The sun and moon eclipsed, the unity ...
was me, who wandered ... distillations
of the red redeeming [tincture] of life
and light to find joy ... universe is magical
and its bodies lovely mysteries ...

In the morning three apples were picked
From the tree of knowledge
And brought to him for his meal.
He turned one in his hand,
The two sides of the apple
Were faces of the moon
One invisible, one visible,
The secret of life and death.

She carried three apples as gifts
From the tree of life.
He understood their meaning
And ate—
The fruit dropped from the tree, leaves
Turned and fell, as did he—
The body was burnt on a pyre
Whose flames returned to the sun.

38. *Stair of Iris*

The blackness of the river bottom rises
From the shadow. [Sweat] of the earth evaporates.
All things come together in a whorl: the earth
The waves of the river and damp air.
Elements unite then move apart ...
Never ceasing their exchange.

... reflection of the sun on clouds.
Clouds gather. The white south wind brings
Rain ... flows around the clouds
And pounds the fields of Aphrodite
Then in the calm afterwards, colors
Soothe the bruised sky.

... [rainbow] ... stairway for Iris
To bring messages from the gods—now
[it] is the message. The earth
Is at its end. All things are connected
In harmony. The burnished
River deflecting blades of light ...
Blackness descends again.

29. *Aeakus humbled*

You had perfect wings
silken, new, ten-ribbed, white—
we tore them off—
on the cinder path . . .
under cavernous air.
You cried but could not move
in the absence of wings.

You had perfect eyes,
blue—no gold—and piercing—
they could make us move
or burn ours out—
we tore them out
. . . left you under the bridge
by the river of oblivion.

"Mother, father, crippled judges
can you take away my perfect heart?"

30. *Amaryllis*

I saw you under moonlight and you
Reflected me. I saw you under starlight
And you grew distant and mysterious:
Your skin was the color of evening
As if you breathed that color in
And pumped the blood of sky through
Your flesh—your nipples were darker
Than your breasts—your hair a deeper
Blue—your eyes . . . aurora lights.

I saw you again in the forest by day
Standing under the cedars
Swaying before me in green—
Your body was a tender shoot
Nourished by the blood of leaves.
Your limbs were lighter than
Your body, as if newly grown
And your face about to bloom.

I held out my arms to you
But you turned and ran
And changed as you did: Clay
And dirt made you red and brown
Rocks on the cliff turned you grey;
You looked back once as you fell
Through air—

39. *Eleusius*

... dusky ... down sweating stairs
to the cave ... torches ... a shadow
carried the basket forward and turned
the cloth ... she jerks backwards staring—
what thing ... [?]   horror? [glory?]
had she prepared for with fasts and visions
agonized and glorious
she left closed-mouthed as she had sworn [to].
there is no secret unless one keeps it.
... no secret ...

40. *Medusa*

Truth has more value buried
for who can look upon its naked
aspect unparalyzed? ... who can
look upon the medusa face of truth?

Like Perseus, we must view truth
in the mirror of words ...
its reflection distorted by myth—
or see its shadow at night

40.1 *Sisyphus Free*

... knowledge accustoms us to failure ...
failure to obscurity ....

most successful, for the unbearable weight
he has been told to push, he has pushed aside

observing the order of life ... he smiles
the stone rests at the bottom of the hill

41. Odysseus

I was under contract to a truth
I did not know. I fought great battles
With myself ... purified myself
With violence and longing.

All things have been wedded in memory
And the source of all these, you,
Telemachus and even Argus. I had
To journey home, a symbolic journey
Like that of birds in a cage.
Home can only be approached from [a] distance
... spiraling around the center,
Returning, reordering the chaos of choice.

I spent years in Circe's bed. I left
After exhausting everything but the memory
Of home. I long for home and comfort
And death.
My faith is such that even burdened [with age]
And wrinkled, I will plant seedling trees.

42. *Penelope*

… not Odysseus we praise
but Penelope, not the adventurous braveteer
but the woman constant and clear
…
not he who takes exceptions, not he
who ever roams, but the [keeper] of homes,
the center …
not inspiration, not the prodigal son,
but she who perseveres
not one marvelous action, not the sudden
tide, but the river flowing and calm,
the water steady and near

43. *Horn of Amaltheia*

the child raised …
on the milk of the goat raised the goat
… to the skies …
Capricorn … [like] drops of milk.
One horn was left on earth
filled with food and drink …

then [the] horn … broken into rings
for ornament.

men still plow fields and plant
trees … ignorant of wasted riches …

44. *Pythagoras*

Kneeling on the ground Pythagoras looked up
pointing a grimy finger, "triangle"

"That is not a triangle, Pythagoras,
it is only dirt."

"Now, it is more than dirt—
it holds the [form] of a triangle."

45. *Socrates*

Socrates, be quiet
and learn to listen to what is not-man
as well as [to what is]

... see the foundation on which [all rests]
... the connections between ...

the examined life, lived [behind walls],
is not [worth] living

46. *Daphne*

... from the laurel your body bends
towards me, your arms like vines
wrap me and root me in the earth.

The chase is reversed and we become
human at last ...

Natural Philosophy: Great World Order

1.	**Particles**

1.0	The universe is composed of particles
1.0.1	The particles are all identical
1.0.2	Each is whole
1.0.4	...uncuttable...

1.1	solid and full ... not acted ... compressed
1.1.1	... full extension ...
1.1.4	indivisible because of the smallness of size ... incommensurable as the diagonal of a square

1.2.	... are uncreated ...
1.2.2	particles cannot be changed ... substance of nature (*phusis*)

1.3	shaped like spheres

1.4	particles are forms (*eidola*)
1.4.2	...can only think of how they are and call our thoughts ideas of forms

1.5	untouchable [but also] indescribable and [maybe] unimaginable

2.	**Nothingness**

2.0	... exists as much as any thing ...not real not less than real

2.1	nothing is of necessity
2.1.2	nothing not-exists ... it allows existence
2.1.3	... outlines a thing ...makes it possible

2.2	nothing is not the black shadow on the river bottom nor the darkness lying in caves ...not any object

4.1.1   ... account for the infinite variety of the universe
4.1.2   variety with limits ...
4.1.3   chance manipulates ...

4.2   like letters of the alphabet particles have no significance of their own [individually]
4.2.1   ... their order [taxis] and position [thesis] ... into aggregates with different meanings

4.3   three differences in the particles—rhythm, touching, and turning—are reflected in the variety of things seen
4.3.1.1   rhythm is the internal arrangement of the inseparable parts ... [the] shape
4.3.1.2   touching is the position ... regard to other particles
4.3.1.3   turning ... regard to itself
4.3.2.1   "A" differs from "N" in rhythm
4.3.2.2   [AN]...differs from "NA" in touching
4.3.2.3   "Z" differs from "N" in turning
4.3.3   ... differences account for infinite [variety] ...

4.4   reality is not the being of things ... [but] their becoming and unbecoming in the flow of particles

4.5   ... builds up layers from ... to clumps of particles to the bodies of things as a ship's hull is constructed ...

4.6   ... exist that cannot be seen
4.6.1   ... dancing of particles in a sunbeam is indication of the movement of other particles hidden to sight ... propelled by the impact of invisible blows
4.6.2   characteristics from the motion ... visible and invisible ...

4.7.3   restlessness shakes the foundation of our senses

4.8   things fall apart ...
4.8.1   motion ... carries it out of its aggregate
4.8.2   ... uniqueness of the body changes

5. Cosmogony

5.0   [The] universe is not alive nor governed by foresight or design ... put together by particles ...

5.0.1   ... necessity of physical cause without purpose

5.1   ... void distended with large numbers of moving particles which through their motions may form in a single whirl where they collide and circle in all sorts of ways and then separate

5.1.1   ... own laws ... commotion attracts more particles and from their whirl a cosmos is formed

5.1.2   universes are produced this way ... like joining like

5.1.5   ... vortex has three stages

5.2.1   the vortex affects all particles uniformly but they retain their original motions and collide and circle. They act like pebbles on the shore cast together by waves of their own motion ... separated by size as large stones are driven to the same place [together] round and round as if their [similarity] had an attractive force

5.2.2   one direction is equal to the tendency in any other but the direction of the vortex produces a congestion that impedes motion ... smaller particles are squeezed out toward the outer void while larger ones stay behind uniting their motions into the first spherical body. This membrane stands apart from the movement of the surrounding universe as an individual formation.

5.2.3   [The] vortex is like an eddy of water ... particles are not rigid like a rotating shield nor disconnected. Larger slower particles become more compact and form an earth ... motion stronger at its outer edge. The outer part of the membrane is thinned forming a halo ... occurs between the central body and outer membrane

5.2.4   The outer membrane spins off particles and collects others from the outer universe ... finest bodies—air and dust—are contact between inner and outer

5.2.5   ... universes are created this way

36

5.3   the center is everywhere in each separate thing and related to all other centers

5.4   all of these things—earth, sea, and sun—are in tune with their parts

5.5   creation growth decay and destruction are the stages of the history of a compound body ... solid particles colliding with it do not destroy it, then the internal shifting of its own may change it.

5.5.1   the changing object is both the same and not the same because particles enter and leave unnoticed ... form distorts slowly.

5.5.2   change is the slow regularity of exchange of particles from a vortex with its surroundings

5.5.3   aggregations ... give a universe its stability

5.6   ... order has its coming into being so it has its waxing waning and destruction according to necessity ...

5.7   order is the birth of chaos
chaos is the birth of order ... [and] they play

5.7.1   with vision we make order to change chaos
but vision illuminates the chaos clearly

5.8   particles form a rhythm with nothing that carries through order and disorder [as] through mystery and reason

5.10   stars are independent and haphazard ... there is no perfection in the crystal sphere unless it belongs in the mind of the seer.

5.10.1   [The] eye contributes to the star ... light of stars hold vast ranges of order that we may rearrange into new constellations over the same stars

5.10.2   ... Scythians know nothing of the milk maid [pattern].

5.11	the secret geometry of chaos cannot be described by any order nor simplified by names or numbers nor reduced to particles in the void
5.11.3	The wild sky sings ... the air and light ... not [simple] colliding particles ... chaos lives!
5.12	reality does not pass out of being even if we no longer see

6. The Nature of the Universe

6.0	the nature of particles and nothing cannot be explained
6.0.1	chance is the primary ... [of] the universe but it is not supreme
6.0.2	... necessity ...
6.1	compound bodies ... not mere aggregates of particles but new entities displaying [qualities] that individual particles do not possess
6.1.1	... quantity produces quality.
6.1.2	qualities leap from numbers of particles
6.2	... different cosmos as in a vortex ... assumes a certain conformation
6.2.1	... exist because individual motions conform to a basic pattern corresponding to laws by ... ruled
6.2.2	new laws can be made ...
6.3	nature is born to matter
6.3.1	matter is the mother of life
6.3.2	... life reaches ...
6.4	change is wrought by repetition by repetition and motion everything leads to its own [transcendence or emergence]
6.5	... no original nature before the rushing of particles ... no original state or golden age

6.5.1	...what [exists that] is still original? [patterns?]
6.6	particles remember each collision ...act differently
6.6.4	past is carried into the present by the flow ...
6.7	yet nature dismantles our history with its motion
6.8	earth water and air are as ever-changing as fire
6.8.2	... sphere of glass ... half disassembled
6.8.3	perfection cannot exist
6.9	the imperfect symmetry of a spider's web is a compromise between simplicity and complexity ... [as well as] constancy and variability
6.9.1	Perfect symmetry is violated in a precise way according to laws just as strict.
6.9.2	... controlled imperfection is the [hallmark] of reality
6.9.3	... dislodge perfection as the form of nature.
6.10	imperfect geometry of nature is the cage of life and we do not see the cage
6.10.1	[yet] we complete the cage with [our] laws of perfection.
6.10.2	we value order for the same reason we value [shitting] regularly—it is necessary for life
6.11.2	indistinct shadow that surrounds an image
6.12	day and night are a rhythm
6.14	the earth is already old if each year were a heartbeat it would still be far older than our ancestors' history.

7.   The Nature of Perception

7.0   why is there not just void?
        because nothing cannot appear whole to a part of it
        ... we are parts ... see things in part

7.1   qualities perceived by the senses exist by convention,
        by our opinion, and by our theories ...
        monsters formerly seen are seen no more
        ... new things loom.
7.1.1   elements exist as primary by nature and all others
        are derivative properties differing from one another
        according to position, order, and shape.
7.1.2   ... but they are no less real and true

7.2   all sensation occurs through contact (*haphe*)
7.2.1   particles flow from things into the pores of the eyes
7.2.2   these images are similar in shape to the surface of
        the visible object
7.2.2.1 we only see outsides ...
7.2.2.2 a film falls into the eye of the observer becoming an
        image

7.3   images—violet-like—show us true being

7.4   ... see more than others
7.4.1   [the] universe appears different to different observers
7.4.2   ... our senses fit reality

7.5   ... two levels of existence
7.5.1   imperceptible particles have no qualities at all
7.5.2   through the touch of aggregations of particles in the
        void plants and animals appear, yellow ... smooth or
        rough

7.6   Infinite arrangements of dull uncounted identical
        particles accounts for the wealth of experience

7.7	The universe achieves unity as it passes through the [animal/plant] body.
7.8	... perceptions cannot cause wisdom since they are often incomplete or contradictory
7.9	... arise from absences or oppositions as when we feel cold without heat or smooth without rough
7.10	Senses are alterations of a body to its surroundings ...

8.   The Nature of the Mind and Soul

8.0	... thought is a sensation
8.0.1	thinking is the same species as perception ... the whole body takes a part in thought
8.0.2	thought takes place ... forms come from outside ... neither sensation or thought can begin without the forms of things impinging ...
8.1	[men] think new thoughts every day
8.1.1	... mind can compound thought with memory and emotion
8.1.2	why are the sick creative?
8.2	The universe is held together by memory but everything is renewed by forgetting
8.2.3	instincts of animals are truer guides than human appetites—an animal knows how much it needs, but a man does not
8.3.1	we are pupils of the animals in the most important arts—spinning building and singing
8.3.2	we are inferior to animals in strength and swiftness we can barely swim and jump [much less] fly
8.3.3	we can imitate all of the animals and that is our most unique skill and unparalleled strength [imitation].

41

8.6   the universe ... by accidental cause but we may react with some degree of rational choice as opposed to panic or [automation]

8.6.1   some have fabricated an image of chance as an excuse for their own stupidity but chance rarely conflicts with intelligence which can set many things in order

8.6.2   the shuffling of particles is automatic and blind but their sorting is a prerogative of rational minds

8.7   human understanding is a new layer of order in nature

8.8   ... [my] head is like a thundercloud where ideas flash and disappear leaving only bare tracks for memory.

8.9   ... in a doorway between opposites—earth and sky life and death

8.9.1   we even know by twos ... joy and suffering, freedom and ...

8.9.2   opposites are in rhythm and the rhythm is one ...

8.10   ... not to boast of victory or weep at defeat all things change by day ... rhythm holds the universe in its [sway]

8.11   sleep is caused by relaxation ... body activity

8.11.1   flesh of dreams flesh of life ... chilled or heated ... fits the whole

8.11.2   Dreaming distills the wine of life ... may reveal hidden meaning

8.11.3   ... hopes ... of the day ... fitting in new patterns ... perception turned inward ... We are surprised by particles because of unexpected depth of ... patterns

8.12   things are a pattern of particles life is a pattern of things thought is a pattern of life, and the soul is ... [pattern of thought]

8.12.2	the soul is corporeal like the nature of fire
8.12.3	... [if the] soul exists then it must be more delicate than life and thought and more easily destroyed
8.12.6	The soul is made and cared for by the soil, like a tree
8.13	sleep belongs to the body death belongs to the body and the soul
8.14	death ... [not] breathing
8.14.1	death takes place when the pattern of particles is disrupted ... [as] by a sword stroke
8.14.2	we owe our lives to death. it is the salt to moments and saves them from being tasteless

Aphrodite Astra

On the Nature of Man

9.   Ethics

9.0   Happiness is the best reason for living.
9.0.1   [happiness] is achieved through the right
          techniques of living
9.0.2   ... place for play and surprise

9.1   physical pleasures are primary
9.1.1   ... give well-being
9.1.2   purest pleasure is balance (*isonomia*) that results
          from the absence of pain ... presence of virtues
          ... prudence

9.2   the most human fault is sloth ... where the mind ac-
          cepts only one cause one quality or one perspective

9.3   immoderate desire is the mark of a child

9.4   ethics is a habitual way of life

9.5   emulate the deeds of virtue and not the words

9.6   ... must revere what is common to all [and] what is
          unique ... particles as well as gold the earth
          as well as the body's beauty ... life as well as
          the form and color of statues
9.6.3   How can beauty be explained? Anything of beauty
          can be destroyed by taking it apart, although
          the parts may have a beauty of their own.
9.6.5   the wealth of a country ...
9.6.6   our will alters the country as well as the flow ...

9.7   there are no goals in life ... no heights to be
          attained once; there is only balance in relation

9.8	life is not a preparation for death ... it is an experiencing of ... patterns ... the music is played not saved for the end
9.9	meaning itself flows loosely
9.10	as patterns of particles change thus the laws governing them change
9.11	we make laws for ourselves
9.12	greatest joy is to stand quietly ... understand the flow
9.13	those who would have serenity of spirit should choose a few moderate activities within their capacity and strive for reasonable fullness
9.14	happiness and unhappiness are properties of the soul and do not come from cattle or gold
9.15	those who persuade are more effective [than] those who enforce laws
9.15.1	one who is prevented from doing wrong by law may learn ... secretly but ... by duty may do right openly through understanding
9.15.2	families do not need laws ... but in cities [do] ...
9.16	many sacrifice pleasures to live long yearning for what is absent but neglecting what enjoyments they have
9.17	in avoiding death one spends a long time dying
9.20	... for all to bear some [loss] than for some to bear all
9.21	Freedom of speech is a sign of freedom but freedom is worthless unless the speech has content [intelligence]
9.22	One must avoid speaking and writing of evil deeds.

This increases the disposition to [crime] as certainly as association with [criminals].

9.23   ... a reasonable man tries to control desires and not fight them and accepts that he cannot have perfect control.

9.26   To the wise, the whole earth is open.
The native [place] of a good
soul is the whole earth (see 247. Freeman)

9.26.1 life carries many necessary conditions. The wise man recognizes which to change and which to submit ...

9.26.2 ... can [potential] ...

9.27   The good of youth [are] strength and beauty
the [best] of age is moderation (see 294. Freeman)

9.28   ... human life is brief and weak and mixed with difficulties. Realize this and keep happy with moderate desires and possessions.

10.   Economics

10.1   ... poverty and wealth are relative and may be measured in time or money accomplishments thoughts feelings perceptions beauty or appreciation ...

10.2   Greed is a fever that burns awareness

10.3   only man is vain enough to build walls to keep out wind and waves

10.4   only man is vain enough to claim water and land and not keep account of them

10.5   who owns rock and fire and water?
we share only what passes through us

10.6   labor gives meaning to those who cannot imagine one
... the wise labor to attain meaning and find pleasure

10.7   The [lust] for wealth, unless [ruled] by satisfaction,
is far more painful than poverty; greater passions create greater needs. (see 219. Freeman)

10.8   ... a sensible person bears poverty well

10.9   A rich accumulation is provided by luck. Sufficiency
comes from foresight.

11.   Politics

11.0   Societies are formed, like all other cosmos, through aggregations in a vortex.

11.0.1   ... they continue to exist because individual motions
within them conform in the main to a single pattern
or group of patterns corresponding to the written
or unwritten laws by which they are governed

11.0.2   social patterns are subject to change because of the
movement of all ... [things]

11.1   laws are necessary in any civilized community

11.2   Women rulers had the same faults as men

11.3   laughter is ... fundamental freedom

11.4   nature is unfair

11.5   justice retreated the moment she was born ...
Astrea fled

11.6   the gods took both sides in the Trojan war

11.7   one must give the greatest importance to the affairs of state. The well-run state works for the common good and this is the greatest protection for [its] citizens.

11.8   One must not respect the opinion of others more or less than one's own—one's own opinion must stand as the law of one's soul

12.   Education

12.0   Many should not have children. There are great risks: success is rare and attended by care and strife; failure means unbearable grief . . .

12.1   any [one] can love a baby but few see beyond the [drooling]

12.2   Nature and education are similar. Education transforms and in transforming creates . . .

12.4   Learning is preparation for seeing . . . is comprehension of what is seen. Wisdom is appropriate action . . . Karmines knows everything about philosophy, but he is not wise.

12.5   Wisdom is not the automatic fruit of age but the product of experience and understanding

12.5.1   . . . the weed teaches the same lesson as the cedar . . .

12.6   . . . complete knowledge embraces all sources . . . perception to memory thought belief and theory

12.6.3   Heraklitus asked me yesterday about the truth. I replied [that] it depended on whether we were walking under trees or through a river.

| 12.7 | Do we add to what we see or distill it from perception? |
| 12.7.2 | ... the earth is accretional ... history is distilled |

12.8	... can one only learn at Crotona [the academy] ?
12.8.1	There are many kinds of wisdom beyond the theoretical and the practical
12.8.2	... nature is the most constant teacher.

| 12.9 | the injured Vulcan became armorer to the gods, indispensable ... are specialists [all] crippled? ... |

13.   Religion

13.2	To jump into a volcano is not the act of a god ... but to return is ... [and] who has seen Empedokles lately?
13.2.1	... colossal ... front of deep craters ... turbulent black flames
13.2.2	Who would I worship? Zeus and power? Aphrodite and love? ... the wind ... or Chronos and time? —for time holds all power and love

| 13.3 | If a fish cannot imagine legs and a frog cannot imagine wings then how can we imagine gods without than eyes and hands? |

| 13.4 | The gods evaporate like clouds they came from nothing and left nothing behind, not thrones or texts or ruins or treasures— what man now petitions their return? if we exist in the image of our creators then we are clouds |

| 13.4.1 | perhaps we [too] are as insubstantial as clouds ... |

13.5   we made gods to go beyond our [own] limits
but then made them [act] human ...

13.6   due to natural causes ... understood ...

13.7   ... to reconcile a misunderstood apartness with a misunderstood absolute ...

13.7.1   particles are absolute and connect us with all things
and the void

13.7.2   ... [religion] is social

13.8   the true temple should be the home ... The muses
work in the home, not the market. Their [droppings]
calcified is what is left and sold.

13.8.1   In writing of abstract particles and free designs [I]
have become anchored to my home and garden—
the human spirit ... emerged too far from
the level of particles to ...

13.8.6   all of nature is home to the good ...

13.9   women anguish when men die in war or their children
are taken by disease or famine but ... children will go
to war ... [everyone] dies ...

13.10   the obligation to exist ... [drives life]

13.11   reverence is the acknowledgment of the necessity
of death

13.11.1 the dead participate in all things

13.11.2 ... life feeds on life.

13.12   the whole is whole with nothing outside
we ascend within ...

13.13   we intend some unseen end ... not fire or mind
... some distant [realizeable] completion

Genuine Fragments

14.1   the moon blocks the sun the earth blocks ...
        therefore ... moon nearer to the sun

14.2.1 Scorpio: fourth day—Pleiades set at dawn, leaves
        begin to fall. Cold winds

14.2.2 Pisces: fourth day—halcyon days
        fourteenth day—bird winds blow cold

14.2.3 Gemini: fourteenth day—sun explodes in flames
        twenty-ninth day—Orion rises

15.1   Cassandra doubly torments herself, by remembering
        and by anticipating ... that is her punishment
        by being [true] and unheard ... or made [false]

16.   the voice of fire travels in air
        air has its roots in rock and rock ... water
        ... water is empty

17.1   the worm completes the fruit ...

19.   one direction is toward multiplicity ... this is
        the way of life and thought

19.2   [other] is the way of unity to the level
        of completeness and death

19.3   particles move from unity to multiplicity and back again

20.   we can never take anything completely apart ...
        [or be] able to put it back together

20.1   ... proper way of knowing to observe ... at a natu-
        ral pace in a natural setting ... dialectically [synthesize
        things] in our selves ... [by dissociation]

21.1   we lose ourselves in images ... burn our [brains]
        with their brightness emitting blasts of sparks
        that fade ... the best turn to cinders in days.

22.1   so many parts of our maps are blank ...
        perhaps the most valuable [places]

23.0   nothing is true but the [all-present] from which
        the past diverges and where the future converges
23.0.2 nothing is absolute not even particles
23.0.3 the core and the surface are the same
23.0.4 the waters of Lethe close over original thought

24.0   where are these theoretical particles?
        where is the evidence of things not seen?
        the substance of the hoped for ... in the mind?

25.0   art does not reveal an order beneath chaos but
        makes [order] above it
25.1   music arises from superfluity
25.2   human song is an imitation of the song of the void
        ... silence and [waves] interchanged

26.0   I am not a mystic like Archegonus
        mysticism is only a path, not the only one;
        it cannot dominate, only guide
        ... from a common ground
26.1   mysticism is a product of diet
26.2   let the caduceus be our symbol
        as mystery is based on knowledge based
        on mystery ... through all levels
        in an ever-recurring spiral

27.0   ecstasy is a heart which the sun distends

28.0   one records the most profound meanings
        the most ecstatic visions clumsily ... occasionally
        in fragments

About the Author

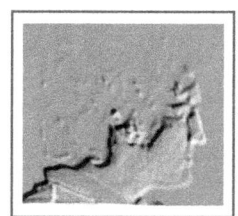

A. M. Caratheodory was born at the time of the largest solar eruption ever recorded—a fact he discovered when he became interested in astronomy. After basic schooling in Virginia, he attended the University of Virginia at Charlottesville, where he studied astrophysics. His work on mathematical models of stars received awards from NSF, NASA, USN, USAF, Goddard Institute, and Bausch & Lomb, among others.

Dropping out of school as a conscientious objector and peace activist, he was drafted. He enlisted in the Air Force, working as a microwave researcher, satellite track technician, medical corpsman, and janitor. After an honorary discharge, he worked as an observer, research assistant, then research associate in astrophysics for a number of installations, including Cambridge Research Labs, Lunar and Planetary Lab, and Steward Observatory.

After three federal budget cuts suggested a change in careers, he worked at a series of jobs that included artist's model, lifeguard, truck driver, dishwasher, gardener, bookstore clerk, library supervisor, gymnastics teacher, printer, book editor, opera set painter, animal hospital attendant, television repairman, auto mechanic's apprentice, and computer engineer.

Returning to school, he took courses in anthropology, economics, psychology, biology, and ecology, before returning to work in astrophysics. He works as a consultant for an observatory in Chile, where he is also a forest activist in the Beech forests of Tierra del Fuego.

Finding that his experience followed Auden's prescription for poets, he has written in poetic, as well as scientific, forms. He has been published in numerous local, regional, and international journals; since 1984, he has worked only on book-length themes. Fragments was a finalist in the National Poetry Series for 1994. He continues to work hard to keep to the dictates of Wordsworth and Novalis to be a good poet.

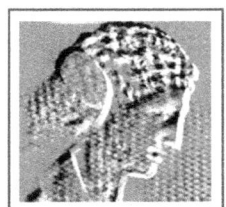

Fragments

A. M. Caratheodory

Colophon

Cover:	A. M. Caratheodory
Collages:	A. M. Caratheodory
Design:	Rian Ecological—REDesigns
Graphics:	M. C. de Passe
Text type:	Gill Sans
Display type:	Papyrus
Programs:	PageMaker, Photoshop
Computer:	Mac Performa 6400

21.1   we lose ourselves in images ... burn our [brains]
        with their brightness emitting blasts of sparks
        that fade ... the best turn to cinders in days.

28.0   one records the most profound meanings
the most ecstatic visions clumsily ... occasionally
in fragments

www.ingramcontent.com/pod-product-compliance
Lightning Source LLC
Chambersburg PA
CBHW071216130626
46555CB00004B/1732